PATHWAYS OF FAITH

ILLUSTRATIONS BY ROGER SPEER

Forward Movement
Cincinnati, Ohio

ISBN: 9780880284370

Printed in USA

COLOR YOUR JOURNEY: *PATHWAYS OF FAITH*

A drawing can be a powerful tool. Jesus draws in the dirt, teaching a difficult and humbling lesson to a group of people who are about to stone one of their own to death. Scripture tells us he draws a picture, or a word, or something in the sand, and a woman who has been marked for death is allowed to live. Jesus understands the power we have in our hands, the power of what we create and share.

Long before many of us ever picked up a pen or tapped a keyboard to write down what we were feeling or thinking, we picked up crayons to express ourselves. Somewhere along the way, we stopped coloring, intent on more grown-up ways of communicating with the world. *Pathways of Faith* invites people of all ages to re-enter that creative and colorful space while at the same time engaging your faith.

The original illustrations by artist Roger Speer are inspired by some of the best-loved stories in the Bible. You might use this coloring book as a companion to *The Path: A Journey through the Bible. The Path* is the story of the Bible from creation to revelation, excerpted from the New Revised Standard Version and presented in an accessible, easy-to-read format. If there are children in your life, you might read and color together with *The Path: Family Storybook*.

Using your favorite set of colored pencils, make the pictures you find in *Pathways* your own. Color in the lines or outside them. Use traditional colors—or unexpected ones. Use the perforated edges to tear out your creation and hang it on a wall or tuck the book away in a drawer for safekeeping. Whatever way you decide to color and preserve your pictures is the right way. Our prayer is that, as you fill in these pages, your faith in the goodness and greatness of God will increase and that you will find refreshment and rest in this book.

Take a picture of your coloring page and share on Facebook or Twitter with **#PathwaysOfFaith**

GOD SAW THAT IT WAS GOOD

In the beginning when God created the heavens and the earth, the earth was a formless void and darkness covered the face of the deep, while a wind from God swept over the face of the waters. Then God said, "Let there be light."

Genesis 1:1-3

GOD SAW THAT IT WAS GOOD ❧ Genesis 1:1-3

THE SIGN OF THE COVENANT

God said, "This is the sign of the covenant that I make between me and you and every living creature that is with you, for all future generations. I have set my bow in the clouds, and it shall be a sign of the covenant between me and the earth."

Genesis 9:12-13

THE SIGN OF THE COVENANT ⚓ Genesis 9:12-13

THE ANCESTOR OF A MULTITUDE

Look toward heaven and count the stars, if you are
able to count them…So shall your descendants be.
Genesis 15:5

THE ANCESTOR OF A MULTITUDE ❧ Genesis 15:5

JOSEPH HAD A DREAM

Know that I am with you and will keep you wherever you go,
and will bring you back to this land; for I will not
leave you until I have done what I have promised you.
Genesis 28:15

JOSEPH HAD A DREAM ❧ Genesis 28:15

I AM WHO I AM

I have observed the misery of my people who are in Egypt;
I have heard their cry…and I have come down to deliver them
from the Egyptians, and to bring them up out of that land to
a good and broad land, a land flowing with milk and honey.

Exodus 3:7-8

I AM WHO I AM ✍ Exodus 3:7-8

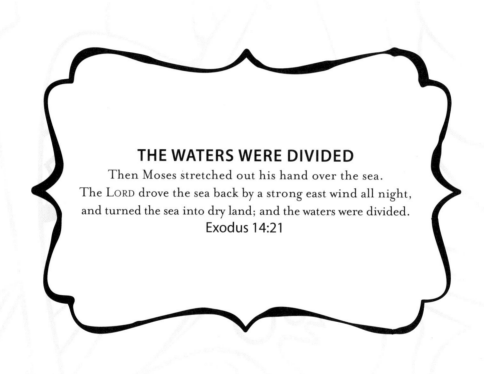

THE WATERS WERE DIVIDED

Then Moses stretched out his hand over the sea.
The LORD drove the sea back by a strong east wind all night,
and turned the sea into dry land; and the waters were divided.

Exodus 14:21

THE WATERS WERE DIVIDED ❧ Exodus 14:21

THE WALL FELL DOWN FLAT

The people said to Joshua, "The LORD our
God we will serve, and him we will obey."
Joshua 24:24

THE WALL FELL DOWN FLAT ⚬ Joshua 24:24

THE LORD RAISED UP JUDGES

The Israelites did what was evil in the sight
of the Lord, forgetting the Lord, their God...
But when the Israelites cried out to the Lord,
the Lord raised up a deliverer for the Israelites.

Judges 3:7, 9

THE LORD RAISED UP JUDGES ❧ Judges 3:7, 9

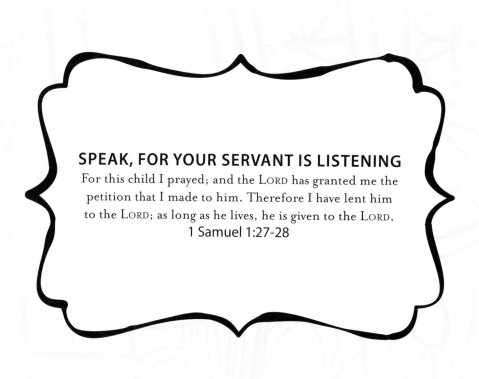

SPEAK, FOR YOUR SERVANT IS LISTENING

For this child I prayed; and the LORD has granted me the petition that I made to him. Therefore I have lent him to the LORD; as long as he lives, he is given to the LORD.

1 Samuel 1:27-28

SPEAK, FOR YOUR SERVANT IS LISTENING ❧ 1 Samuel 1:27-28

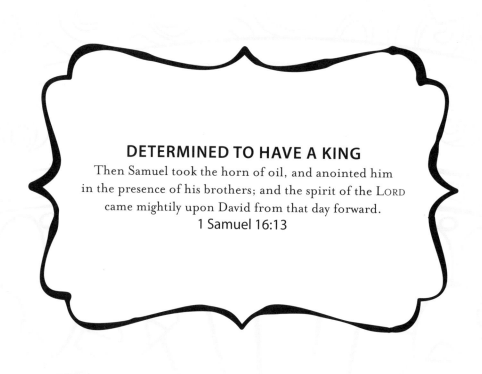

DETERMINED TO HAVE A KING

Then Samuel took the horn of oil, and anointed him
in the presence of his brothers; and the spirit of the LORD
came mightily upon David from that day forward.
1 Samuel 16:13

DETERMINED TO HAVE A KING ❧ 1 Samuel 16:13

A MAN AFTER GOD'S OWN HEART

David said, "The LORD who saved me from the paw of the lion and from the paw of the bear, will save me from the hand of this Philistine." So Saul said to David, "Go, and may the LORD be with you!"

1 Samuel 17:37

A MAN AFTER GOD'S OWN HEART ᕈ 1 Samuel 17:37

THE WISDOM OF GOD WAS IN HIM
"Give your servant therefore an understanding mind
to govern your people, able to discern between good
and evil; for who can govern this your great people?"
It pleased the Lord that Solomon had asked this.
1 Kings 3:9-10

THE WISDOM OF GOD WAS IN HIM 🕮 1 Kings 3:9-10

HERE I AM; SEND ME

Holy, holy, holy is the LORD of hosts;
the whole earth is full of his glory.
Isaiah 6:3

HERE I AM; SEND ME ❧ Isaiah 6:3

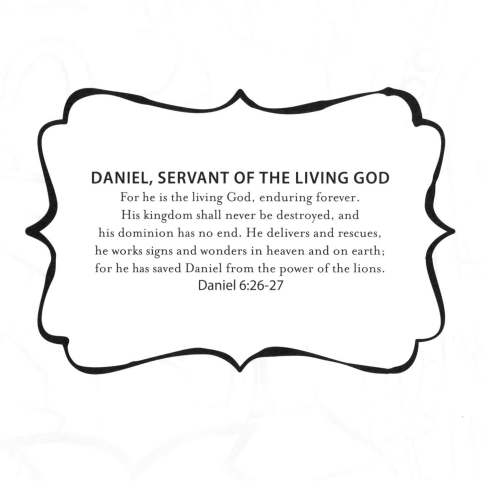

DANIEL, SERVANT OF THE LIVING GOD

For he is the living God, enduring forever.
His kingdom shall never be destroyed, and
his dominion has no end. He delivers and rescues,
he works signs and wonders in heaven and on earth;
for he has saved Daniel from the power of the lions.
Daniel 6:26-27

DANIEL, SERVANT OF THE LIVING GOD ☙ Daniel 6:26-27

GO UP AND REBUILD

When the builders laid the foundation of the temple
of the LORD, the priests in their vestments were stationed
to praise the LORD with trumpets…"For he is good,
for his steadfast love endures forever toward Israel."

Ezra 3:10-11

GO UP AND REBUILD ᐧ Ezra 3:10-11

GOOD NEWS OF GREAT JOY

Then Mary said, "Here am I, the servant of the Lord;
let it be with me according to your word."
Luke 1:38

GOOD NEWS OF GREAT JOY ❧ Luke 1:38

FOLLOW ME

And Jesus said to them, "Follow me and I will
make you fish for people." And immediately
they left their nets and followed him.

Mark 1:17-18

FOLLOW ME ❧ Mark 1:17-18

PROCLAIMING THE GOOD
NEWS OF THE KINGDOM

I am the bread of life. Whoever comes to me will never be
hungry, and whoever believes in me will never be thirsty.
John 6:35

PROCLAIMING THE GOOD NEWS OF THE KINGDOM ❧ John 6:35

CRUCIFY HIM!

Pilate asked him, "So you are a king?" Jesus answered, "You say that I am a king. For this I was born, and for this I came into the world, to testify to the truth. Everyone who belongs to the truth listens to my voice."
John 18:37

CRUCIFY HIM! ❧ John 18:37

WE HAVE SEEN THE LORD

The Lord has risen indeed.

Luke 24:34

WE HAVE SEEN THE LORD 🐾 Luke 24:34

FILLED WITH THE HOLY SPIRIT

Repent, and be baptized every one of you in the
name of Jesus Christ so that your sins may be forgiven;
and you will receive the gift of the Holy Spirit.
Acts 2:38

FILLED WITH THE HOLY SPIRIT ❧ Acts 2:38

GRACE MAY ABOUND

Rejoice always, pray without ceasing, give thanks
in all circumstances; for this is the will of
God in Christ Jesus for you.
1 Thessalonians 5:16-18

GRACE MAY ABOUND 1 Thessalonians 5:16-18

BE DOERS OF THE WORD

You must understand this, my beloved: let everyone
be quick to listen, slow to speak, slow to anger.

James 1:19

BE DOERS OF THE WORD ❧ James 1:19

THE ALPHA AND THE OMEGA

Holy, holy, holy,
the Lord God the Almighty,
who was and is and is to come.
Revelation 4:8

THE ALPHA AND THE OMEGA ❧ Revelation 4:8

THE PATH

In all your ways acknowledge him,
and he will make straight your paths.
Proverbs 3:6

THE PATH ~ Proverbs 3:6

WAYS TO USE *PATHWAYS OF FAITH*

Begin on any page you like—whichever picture you want to color first is the exact right place to start. We recommend that you use colored pencils for optimal results.

Consider using this book in tandem with your daily devotional habits. The illustrations correspond to the chapters of *The Path: A Journey through the Bible* and *The Path: Family Storybook*, and the scripture passages on the left-hand side of the page illuminate each illustration. *Pathways of Faith* also can be a wonderful companion to the daily devotionals of *Forward Day by Day, Saint Augustine's Prayer Book*, or any other resource you may use to focus your time with God. You might set aside five minutes of "coloring time" before or after your reading and prayer time.

Take *Pathways of Faith* with you during the day, in your backpack, diaper bag, shoulder bag, briefcase, or purse. Don't forget your pencils! Reward yourself during a coffee or lunch break with some coloring; share a picture with a coworker across the table or cubicle wall.

Make one of your book club nights a coloring night. Or start a new book club that is for coloring. It can be a wonderfully relaxing way to spend time with friends and make new ones!

If you really like one of your pictures, share it with us on Facebook or Twitter by tagging it with **#PathwaysOfFaith**. With perforated edges, the pictures are easy to pull out and frame for posterity, tack on your fridge, or give to your mom to put up on hers.

If you want to see how the artist created and painted the illustrations, they are available in full color in *The Path: Family Storybook*. You may want to pick up a copy of *The Path* or the *Family Storybook* (available at www.ForwardMovement.org) and color your way through reading the Bible.

Enjoy this book. We are pleased and proud to offer you this resource to inspire your own growth as a disciple of Jesus and to empower you in spreading the good news of his love.

ABOUT THE ILLUSTRATOR

Roger Speer is a lifelong servant of the Episcopal Church. He has served with mission, congregational, diocesan, national, and international formation initiatives during an exciting tenure as a youth minister. At heart, Roger is an artist and craftsman. He holds degrees in art education and graphic design, as well as various training certifications that he uses to produce new ways to express the gospel with as much innovation as possible. He is husband to Fran and father to Fynn.

ABOUT FORWARD MOVEMENT

Forward Movement is committed to inspiring disciples and empowering evangelists. While we produce great resources like this book, Forward Movement is not a publishing company. We are a ministry.

Our mission is to support you in your spiritual journey, to help you grow as a follower of Jesus Christ. Publishing books, daily reflections, studies for small groups, and online resources is an important way that we live out this ministry. More than a half million people read our daily devotions through *Forward Day by Day*, which is also available in Spanish (*Adelante Día a Día*) and Braille, online, as a podcast, and as an app for your smartphones or tablets. It is mailed to more than fifty countries, and we donate nearly 30,000 copies each quarter to prisons, hospitals, and nursing homes. We actively seek partners across the Church and look for ways to provide resources that inspire and challenge.

A ministry of the Episcopal Church for eighty years, Forward Movement is a nonprofit organization funded by sales of resources and gifts from generous donors.

To learn more about Forward Movement and our resources, visit us at www.ForwardMovement.org or www.VenAdelante.org.

We are delighted to be doing this work and invite your prayers and support.

Forward Movement is committed to inspiring
disciples and empowering evangelists.
Visit us at www.ForwardMovement.org
for more resources for your journey.